PENGUIN YOUNG READERS LICENSES
An Imprint of Penguin Random House LLC

Copyright © Anna E. Dewdney Literary Trust. Copyright © 2017 Genius Brands International, Inc.
lished by Penguin Young Readers Licenses, an imprint of Penguin Random House LLC, 345 Hudson Street, New York, New York 10014.
Manufactured in China.

ISBN 9781524783921   10 9 8 7 6 5 4 3 2

llama llama and friends

Based on the bestselling children's book series by Anna Dewdney

llama llama and friends ™

Based on the bestselling children's book series by Anna Dewdney

Anna Dewdney

Illustrated by JJ Harrison

Penguin Young Readers Licenses
An Imprint of Penguin Random House

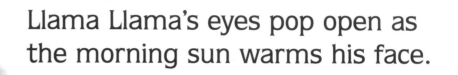

Llama Llama's eyes pop open as the morning sun warms his face.

He hops into his overalls and rushes downstairs. Mama Llama needs his help today.

"Mama," Llama asks,
"is your list ready?"

"Breakfast before errands," says Mama Llama, spooning
out his oatmeal. "Little helpers need lots of energy!"

After breakfast, Llama ties a basket to his scooter. He tucks in Fuzzy with the list. "Let's go!"

Dion dances over.
"QUACK! QUACK!"
"I'll be home soon,"
Llama tells him.
"You keep Mama
company."

Llama sings as he zooms along.

At the store, he bumps into his friend Euclid.
"Hey, Llama. I'm buying a puzzle," says Euclid.
"What are you shopping for?"

Llama checks his list. "Streamers. Why would Mama need them?"
"Hmm." Euclid blinks, thinking hard. "To fancy up your front
yard? Or to perk up her pink car?"

Llama and Euclid peek and poke in every aisle.
Finally, they find the streamers.

Euclid pays for his puzzle.
He helps Llama count his coins.

Outside, Euclid says, "Let's do this puzzle together!"
"Later," Llama promises, waving his list.
Then he scooters off down the hill.

At Daddy Gnu's Bakery, Llama's best buddy, Nelly Gnu, flings open the door. "Llama!" she cries. "I need your help! I'm painting a mural."

"Okay," Llama says, taking a brush and dipping it in the paint.
Together they paint pies, pastries, and cupcakes.
After a while, Llama stands back.

"These look yummy!" he says, gazing at their work.

"Oh no!"

"What?" asks Nelly.

"I forgot!" cries Llama.

"I'm here to buy some cupcakes."

He squeezes the box into his basket.

"See you soon," Nelly calls as Llama scooters away.

Llama struggles up What-a-View Hill, huffing and puffing.

It's so . . . much . . . fun having . . . errands . . . to run!

He flops down at the top.
Thump! Thump! Thump! What was that?
Gilroy Goat is kicking a soccer ball against a tree trunk.

"Hi, Gilroy!" Llama greets his classmate.
"It's Gilroy *the Great*!" Gilroy brags, bouncing
the ball off the tree again. "Bet you can't do this!"

Llama just has to try. The score is tied when Llama's list blows past him, carried by a strong breeze.

"My list!" he cries, scooping it up. "Sorry, Gilroy, I have to run!" Llama jumps back on the scooter.

It's so much fun
having errands to run!

Llama zooms back down the hill and slides to a stop at the farm of Gram and Grandpa Llama.
Gram shuts off the tractor. "A visit from Llama!" she exclaims happily.

Llama gives Gram a big hug, and then holds out his list.
"Mama said you have the colored paper that she needs."
"Yes, here it is." Grandpa hands Llama a pile of colorful paper.
"Thanks!" says Llama. He kisses Gram and Grandpa goodbye
and hurries on his way.

It's so much fun
having errands to run!

As Llama passes the park, his good friend
Luna runs over from the slide.
"Llama, can you play?"

"I'm busy getting stuff for Mama," he replies.
"But I'm almost done."

"Flowers," Luna reads from the list. "I'll help you pick some!"
She gathers a bunch of flowers and makes a bouquet.
While Luna picks, Llama plays on the slide, whooping and giggling.

Luna hands Llama the bouquet. He calls, "Thanks, Luna!" and pushes off as fast as he can.

It's so much fun having errands to run!

As he rides by the school,
he glances at the clock.
He's been gone too long!
Mama Llama will be worried!

But when he arrives home, Mama isn't waiting at the gate,
or peeking out the window, or opening the door.
Llama bursts in.

"SURPRISE!"

shouts everyone.
Llama is speechless!

"It's a party for *you*, Llama," Mama says, "to thank you for always being such a good helper!" She gives him a big hug.

THANK YOU, LLAMA!

Everyone helps set up the party supplies that Llama brought home.
Euclid hangs streamers.
Nelly arranges cupcakes.
Luna places flowers in a vase.
And Gilroy makes hats from the colored paper.
"**QUACK! QUACK!**" says Dion, jiggling the balloons.

Llama laughs and puts on a party hat.

My errands are done
and we're ALL having fun!

Llama laughs and puts on a party hat.

My errands are done and we're ALL having fun!